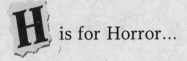**H** is for Horror...

"I know one thing," Dink said. "No ghost is shutting down the Shangri-la if I have anything to do with it!"

"Dink is right," Ruth Rose said. "Mr. Linkletter is our friend. We have to think of something!"

Suddenly the elevator door opened. A figure in white stood staring out at them.

"It's the ghost!" Josh screamed.

The A to Z Mysteries™ series!

The Absent Author
The Bald Bandit
The Canary Caper
The Deadly Dungeon
The Empty Envelope
The Falcon's Feathers
The Goose's Gold
The Haunted Hotel

This one is for Richard.
–R.R.

To the Latchis Hotel.
–J.S.G.

Text copyright © 1999 by Ron Roy
Illustrations copyright © 1999 by John Steven Gurney
All rights reserved under International and Pan-American Copyright Conventions.
Published in the United States by Random House, Inc., New York, and simultaneously
in Canada by Random House of Canada Limited, Toronto.

www.randomhouse.com/kids

Library of Congress Cataloging-in-Publication Data
Roy, Ron
The haunted hotel / by Ron Roy ; illustrated by John Steven Gurney.
p. cm. — (A to Z mysteries)
Summary: When the guests of the Shangri-la Hotel are scared away by a white-haired
female ghost, Dink and his friends investigate the mystery.
ISBN 0-679-89079-3 (trade) — ISBN 0-679-99079-8 (lib. bdg.)
[1. Ghosts—Fiction. 2. Hotels, motels, etc.—Fiction. 3. Mystery and detective stories.]
I. Gurney, John, ill. II. Title. III. Series: Roy, Ron, A to Z mysteries.
PZ7.R8139Hau 1999 98-46856
[Fic]—dc21

Printed in the United States of America   40 39 38 37 36 35

A STEPPING STONE BOOK and colophon are trademarks of Random House, Inc.
A TO Z MYSTERIES and colophon are trademarks of Random House, Inc.

A to Z Mysteries™

The Haunted Hotel

SHANGRI-LA HOTEL

by **Ron Roy**

illustrated by
John Steven Gurney

A STEPPING STONE BOOK™

Random House 🏠 New York

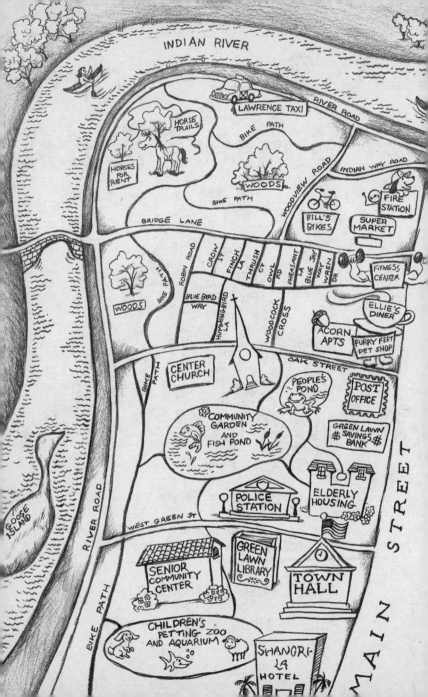

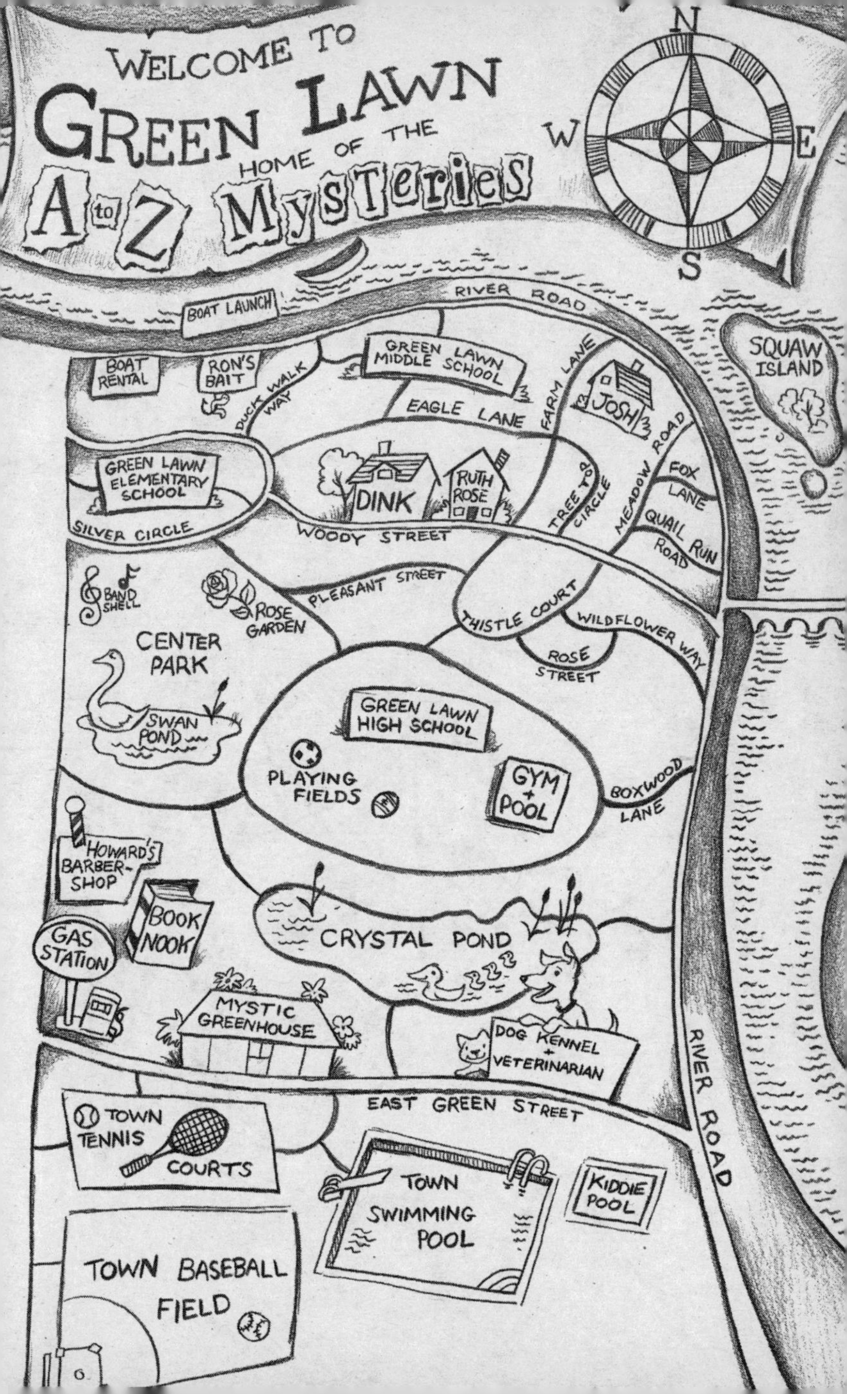

WELCOME TO
GREEN LAWN
HOME OF THE
A to Z MYSTERIES
N
W
E
S
BOAT LAUNCH
RIVER ROAD
GREEN LAWN MIDDLE SCHOOL
BOAT RENTAL
RON'S BAIT
DUCK WALK WAY
EAGLE LANE
FARM LANE
JOSH
SQUAW ISLAND
MEADOW ROAD
GREEN LAWN ELEMENTARY SCHOOL
DINK
RUTH ROSE
TREE TOP CIRCLE
FOX LANE
QUAIL RUN ROAD
SILVER CIRCLE
WOODY STREET
PLEASANT STREET
BAND SHELL
ROSE GARDEN
THISTLE COURT
WILDFLOWER WAY
ROSE STREET
CENTER PARK
SWAN POND
GREEN LAWN HIGH SCHOOL
PLAYING FIELDS
GYM + POOL
BOXWOOD LANE
HOWARD'S BARBER-SHOP
BOOK NOOK
GAS STATION
CRYSTAL POND
MYSTIC GREENHOUSE
DOG KENNEL + VETERINARIAN
EAST GREEN STREET
RIVER ROAD
TOWN TENNIS COURTS
TOWN SWIMMING POOL
KIDDIE POOL
TOWN BASEBALL FIELD

CHAPTER 1

"Oh my gosh!" Dink cried. "There's a ghost in Green Lawn!"

Donald David Duncan, Dink to his friends, was reading the Sunday newspaper on his living room floor.

Josh was sprawled on the sofa. He was using raisins to teach Dink's guinea pig, Loretta, to do math.

Loretta gobbled up one of the raisins.

"Loretta!" Josh scolded. "If you keep eating all the raisins, you'll never learn to add!"

Ruth Rose was doing the crossword puzzle. "Maybe she's trying to teach you to *subtract*, Joshua," she said.

Josh tossed a raisin at her.

"I'm serious, you guys!" Dink said. He poked his finger at the *Green Lawn Gazette*'s front page. "C'mere and read this!"

Ruth Rose glanced at the newspaper. "HEY, THAT'S MR. LINKLETTER!" she yelled.

Josh put Loretta in her cage, then read the headline over Dink's shoulder.

HAUNTED HOTEL! GHOST SCARES AWAY SHANGRI-LA GUESTS

"See, I told you," Dink said.

Josh grinned. "You don't really believe that stuff, do you?" he asked.

"I'll bet it's a Halloween joke or something."

"Yeah, well, Mr. Linkletter looks pretty unhappy in this picture," Dink said. "And he *never* tells jokes!"

"Besides, Halloween isn't for two more weeks," Ruth Rose added.

Josh snorted. "Well, I don't believe in ghosts," he said. "Not until I see one with my own eyes!"

"Listen to this," Dink said, reading from the paper. "'Guests report seeing a ghost floating down the hall at midnight. It was carrying a silver sword!'"

Josh snorted again. "Ghosts don't carry swords," he said.

Ruth Rose reached for her jacket. "Why don't we go to the hotel and see for ourselves?"

"Great idea," Dink said, pulling on his sneakers.

Josh let out a big sigh. "Okay, but

I'm only coming to prove that I'm right."

The kids left Dink's house and headed around Silver Circle.

A bunch of kids were playing soccer at the elementary school. Their noses were pink and Dink could see their breath. The trees surrounding the playing field had turned red and gold.

On Main Street, a long banner hung between two telephone poles. Big letters spelled out the words: GREEN LAWN WELCOMES YOU TO FALL FOLIAGE WEEK, OCTOBER 13–20. COME SEE OUR COLORS!

The kids stopped across the street from the Shangri-la Hotel.

"Look!" Dink said.

People lugging suitcases were streaming out of the hotel. One woman was still wearing her slippers! They were pink and fluffy, with floppy bunny ears.

A newspaper reporter was trying to interview people as they left the hotel.

"Hello, sir," she said to one man. "I'm Linda Gomez from the *Green Lawn Gazette*. What's your reaction to the hotel ghost?"

"No comment!" the man snapped, and hurried away.

"Let's get her to interview *us*," Josh whispered. "Maybe we'll get our names in the paper!"

"We don't know anything yet," Dink said. "Come on, let's find Mr. Linkletter."

The kids crossed the street and squeezed through the crowded doorway. Inside, Mr. Linkletter was standing behind the front desk, listening to a man and woman.

"...and we demand our money back!" the woman was saying. "We came here to see autumn leaves, not to be frightened by ghosts!"

Mr. Linkletter sighed. Dink noticed that his hair was mussed and his eyes were red.

"Of course, Mrs. Caruthers," he said. "You'll get a refund for the entire week. I'm sorry for this trouble. We've never had ghosts at the Shangri-la!"

Dragging their suitcases, the couple hurried past the kids and shoved through the doors.

"Boy, they looked mad," Josh said.

"Let's go talk to Mr. Linkletter," Dink said.

Just then the phone rang. Mr. Linkletter turned to answer it.

"Wait, there's Livvy," Ruth Rose said. "I wonder if she knows anything."

Livvy Nugent was vacuuming the carpet near the elevators. She wore a white uniform with a dark blue apron.

"Hi, Livvy!" Ruth Rose said.

Livvy smiled and switched off the vacuum. "Ruth Rose! The last time I saw you, there was a kidnapping at the hotel. Now we've got a ghost!"

"We read about it in the newspaper," Ruth Rose said. "Is it true?"

"The guests sure think so!" Livvy said. "This place has been a madhouse since Friday night. Our biggest week of the year, and the guests are running out the door!"

Josh smirked. "Does the ghost jump out and say 'boo'?" he asked.

"Josh doesn't believe in ghosts," Ruth Rose said.

"Do *you?*" Livvy asked her.

Ruth Rose shrugged. "I don't know, but *something's* scaring the people away."

"Did you see the ghost?" Dink asked.

Livvy shook her head. "No, and I'd

better not. When ghosts show up, I'm out of here!"

Just then Mr. Linkletter hung up the phone and walked over. "Ms. Nugent, please continue with your work," he said to Livvy.

Then he turned to the kids. "What can I do for you, children?"

"We read about the ghost," Dink said.

Josh rolled his eyes.

"And we saw all the people leaving," Ruth Rose said.

Mr. Linkletter's sad eyes surveyed the lobby. All the guests had left, and the place was empty.

Mr. Linkletter sighed. "Apparently a ghost is scaring away our guests," he said.

"Maybe we can help," Dink said. "Remember how we found Wallis Wallace when you thought she was kidnapped?"

"I'll never forget," Mr. Linkletter said. He looked at the three kids. His thin mustache twitched. His sad eyes squinted.

Finally he said, "Follow me, please." He turned and marched away.

CHAPTER 2

Mr. Linkletter led the kids to his office. The room was small, with just a desk and three chairs. On one wall hung a painting of the hotel. A framed picture of an elderly couple stood on the desk.

"Please sit down," Mr. Linkletter said.

The kids sat. Mr. Linkletter opened a desk drawer and took out a paper bag.

"Mint?" he asked.

Each of the kids took a mint from the bag and popped it into their mouths.

Mr. Linkletter looked inside the bag, then popped a mint into his mouth, too.

He sank back into his chair. "This is terrible," he said.

"Mine tastes okay," Josh said. "I think it's lemon."

Ruth Rose nudged Josh. "I think he means the ghost," she said.

Josh blushed. "Oh, sorry."

"As I was saying," Mr. Linkletter went on, "it all started two days ago, on Friday. It was almost midnight. I was closing my office when a guest ran into the lobby. She was yelling about a ghost on the third floor!"

"Did she say what the ghost looked like?" Dink asked.

Mr. Linkletter smoothed his hair. "She said it was all white—except for the black holes where its eyes should have been!"

The three kids looked at each other. Josh's mouth was hanging open.

Mr. Linkletter rubbed his temples as if he had a headache. "Anyway," he went on, "that guest checked out. Last night, more guests saw the ghost. Again, it appeared at midnight. Today, all those guests checked out."

Mr. Linkletter shook his head. "This ghost is ruining our business!"

"Did any of the guests say where the ghost went after they saw it?" Ruth Rose asked.

"Apparently it just floats away and disappears," he answered.

"Did you see the ghost, too?" Dink asked.

"No. I went upstairs, but all I saw was a dozen terrified guests!"

Mr. Linkletter picked up the picture of the elderly couple on his desk. "This is my aunt and uncle, Florence and Ebenezer Spivets. They've owned the Shangri-la ever since they were first married, forty-seven years ago."

He looked at the kids. "They're very worried. I don't know what will happen to the hotel if this ghost business continues..."

For a minute, nobody said anything. Finally Mr. Linkletter stood up.

"Now, if you'll excuse me," he said, "I have to tell my aunt and uncle that the Shangri-la Hotel won't be having a foliage week this year."

The kids thanked Mr. Linkletter and headed back out into the lobby.

"Guys, we've gotta do something!" Dink whispered.

"But what *can* we do?" Ruth Rose asked.

Just then Livvy hurried over to them. "What'd he say?" she asked.

"He told us about the ghost," Ruth Rose said. She described it for Livvy.

"So there really is a ghost in the hotel!" Livvy said. She looked nervously over her shoulder. "What's Mr. Linkletter gonna do?"

"I don't know," Dink answered. He looked at Josh and Ruth Rose. "But we're gonna try to help, right?"

"Good luck!" Livvy said. "I'll be down in my cubbyhole eating lunch."

She opened a small door next to the elevator and disappeared.

"How're we s'posed to help?" Josh asked Dink. "We don't know anything about ghosts!"

"Well, I know one thing," Dink said. "No ghost is shutting down the Shangri-la if I have anything to do with it!"

"Dink is right," Ruth Rose said. "Mr. Linkletter is our friend. We have to think of something!"

Suddenly the elevator door opened. A figure in white stood staring out at them.

"It's the ghost!" Josh screamed.

CHAPTER 3

The three kids stood frozen as the elevator door slid shut again.

For a minute, no one moved. Then Ruth Rose reached over and punched the UP button for the elevator.

"What're you doing!" Josh squeaked.

"Following the ghost," she said.

"Are you crazy?" Josh said. "What if ghosts don't like kids?"

"Gee, Josh," Dink said. "I thought you didn't believe in ghosts."

"Unless I see one with my own eyes," Josh said, "and I just did! Let's get out of here!" The elevator door opened.

"Too late, Josh," Dink said. He and Ruth Rose pulled Josh into the elevator with them.

Dink pushed the button marked 2. "We'll check each floor," he said.

When the door opened on the second floor, the hallway was empty.

"Two more floors," Ruth Rose said, pushing the number 3 button.

But they didn't see the ghost on the third or fourth floor, either.

"There are no more floors," Dink said, looking at the panel of buttons.

"Good, let's go home!" Josh said.

"What's this one for?" Ruth Rose asked, pointing to a black button without a number.

"Maybe you push it for emergencies," Dink said.

She shook her head. "Nope. This red one says EMERGENCY."

Dink shrugged. "There's only one way to find out," he said. He pushed the black button. The elevator creaked, then slowly started moving up.

"I'm having a nightmare," Josh mumbled. "I'm not really chasing a ghost around a hotel. Any minute, I'm gonna wake up in bed!"

"Don't worry, Josh," Ruth Rose said with a grin. "I'll protect you."

The elevator stopped with a gentle thud.

When the doors opened, the ghost was waiting for them.

"It followed us!" Josh screamed, jumping behind Ruth Rose.

"No, you followed me!" the ghost said. "What do you want?"

Behind the white figure, a door opened. A stooped, gray-haired man stepped into the hall.

The ghost pointed a thin finger at the kids. "They followed me up here, Ebenezer."

The man chuckled and shuffled toward the open elevator. "Well, perhaps we should keep them!"

"NO!" Josh yelled from behind Ruth Rose. "Please let us go! If you kill me, I'll be grounded for sure!"

Dink stared at the figure in white. Where had he seen that face before? Suddenly he remembered. She was the woman in the picture on Mr. Linkletter's desk!

Dink stepped out of the elevator. "Hello, Mr. and Mrs. Spivets," he said. "I'm Dink Duncan and these are my friends Josh and Ruth Rose."

"How d'you do," the man said, peering at Dink. His eyes were the color of blueberries. "You must be the three children our nephew told us about."

Josh peeked at Mrs. Spivets from behind Ruth Rose. "You mean she's not the ghost?" he asked.

"Of course I'm not the ghost!" Mrs. Spivets said. "Ebenezer, shall we invite these three in for cookies?"

"Of course, my love." The old man smiled at the kids. "Come along, kiddos!"

The kids followed Mr. and Mrs. Spivets through a small hallway and into an old-fashioned parlor.

Sunlight poured into the room. Through tall windows, the kids could see treetops across Main Street.

Dink looked around the room. The walls were covered with paintings, and he'd never seen so many books!

Mrs. Spivets came in carrying a

tray. "Please sit," she told the kids. She handed each of them a glass of milk. Her husband bustled in with a cookie jar shaped like a rooster. He pulled off the rooster's head.

"Cookie?" he said.

Each of the kids took one cookie.

"Now then," Mr. Spivets said as he sat next to his wife, "what are you kids up to?"

"We read about the ghost in the newspaper," Ruth Rose said.

"And we came to see it," Dink said.

"But we didn't!" Josh added.

"Then Mr. Linkletter told us how the ghost is ruining the hotel's business," Ruth Rose continued. "So we've decided to investigate!"

Mrs. Spivets stared at the kids. "Investigate?" she said. "Like detectives?"

"Right," Dink said. "Did you see the

ghost?" he asked Mrs. Spivets.

She looked at her husband. "No, but we've heard it, haven't we, dear?"

He nodded. "Two nights in a row! Dreadful noises coming from the walls. And a voice calling out my name! *'Ebenezer,'* it said, *'go away, go away!'*"

Josh gulped. "It knew your name?"

"The voice spoke to me, too," Mrs. Spivets said. "It said, *'Flo, leave this place!'*"

She began to cry into a lace hanky.

Mr. Spivets patted his wife's hand. "We've just made a difficult decision," he told the kids. "We're going to sell the hotel. Some real estate company in New York wants to buy it."

"Sell the Shangri-la!" Dink blurted.

"But you can't!" Ruth Rose said.

"We were going to leave the Shangri-la to our nephew," Mrs. Spivets said. "But now..."

"Now it looks as if the hotel will go to Eatch, Rail, and Roock," Mr. Spivets said.

"Who are they?" Ruth Rose asked.

"They're the three partners in the real estate company," Mr. Spivets said. "They've been after us to sell for months."

He crossed to a small desk and pulled out a letter. "They want to tear down the Shangri-la and build a high-rise in its place!" he said.

Mr. Spivets placed the letter on the tea tray. "Mrs. Spivets and I don't want to sell, but we don't know what else to do. Somehow we feel as if we've failed our guests."

He looked down at his wife. "I telephoned the real estate people this morning. They will be here tomorrow with papers for us to sign."

Mrs. Spivets looked up. Her eyes

were red. "Isn't there anything else we can do?" she asked.

Ebenezer Spivets took his wife's hand in his. "I would do anything for you, dear, but I'm too old to fight ghosts."

"Well, *we're* not!" Dink said, springing to his feet. "We'll find the ghost and get rid of it, too!" He looked at Josh and Ruth Rose. "Right, guys?"

"Right!" Ruth Rose said.

Mr. Spivets beamed. "You're hired!" he said.

Josh groaned. "Can I have another cookie?" he asked.

CHAPTER 4

"How are we gonna get rid of a ghost?" Josh asked in the elevator. "Even if I *did* believe in it."

"I don't know yet," Dink answered. "But we can't let those real estate guys tear down the Shangri-la!"

The elevator door slid open. Mr. Linkletter was standing behind his desk, just staring into space.

"Let's go to my house," Dink whispered. "We can make a plan while we eat."

"Yes!" Josh said. "Those cookies weren't big enough to fill up a flea!"

Dink laughed. "Not everyone has a stomach like the Grand Canyon, Josh!"

They headed up Main Street, then followed Silver Circle around the school to Dink's house.

Dink got out the peanut butter and bread. Josh found a bag of pretzels. Ruth Rose poured milk for everyone.

"Make my sandwich extra fat," Josh ordered. "I'm fainting from hunger!"

Dink pushed the peanut butter and bread toward Josh. "I'm not your servant, your royal highness!"

Josh grinned and began building his sandwich.

"Okay," Dink said, sitting at the table. "How do you get rid of a ghost?"

"First you have to prove that there *is* one," Josh said, taking a big bite of his sandwich.

"You still don't believe there's a ghost at the hotel?" Ruth Rose asked.

Josh swallowed and shook his head. "Nope."

He lined up four pretzels on the table. "We talked to Livvy, but she hadn't seen the ghost," Josh said. He picked up a pretzel and ate it.

"Then we asked Mr. Linkletter if he'd seen the ghost, but he said he hadn't." Josh ate another pretzel.

He picked up the last two pretzels. "Mr. and Mrs. Spivets didn't see the ghost either, they just heard noises!"

Josh popped the pretzels into his mouth. "Guys," he said as he chewed, "nobody we talked to saw the ghost. So maybe there *is* no ghost!"

Dink and Ruth Rose stared at Josh.

"He's right," Ruth Rose said after a minute. "Everyone we talked to said someone *else* had seen the ghost."

"So what should we do?" Dink asked.

"We have to see the ghost for ourselves," Ruth Rose said.

Dink blinked. "But how do we do that?" he asked.

Josh licked peanut butter from his fingers. "Well, we could start by finding someone who really did see the ghost."

"But everyone who saw it checked out of the hotel," Ruth Rose said.

Dink swallowed the last of his sandwich. "We have to talk to those people," he said. "Maybe Mr. Linkletter will help us."

"Good idea," Ruth Rose said. "Let's go back to the hotel."

"No dessert?" Josh asked.

"Wipe off your milk mustache and come on!" Dink said.

The kids hurried back to the hotel. Mr. Linkletter looked up as the kids came in. "I hear you had a chat with my aunt and uncle," he said.

"They hired us to get rid of the ghost!" Dink informed him.

The corners of Mr. Linkletter's mouth wiggled. It was almost a smile. "And do you have a plan?"

"Sort of," Ruth Rose said. "But we need the names and phone numbers of the guests who saw the ghost."

Mr. Linkletter shook his head. "Sorry. Our guests, even the ones who leave, pay for privacy."

"Well, are there any guests left at all?" she asked.

Mr. Linkletter pointed to a man and woman reading in a corner of the lobby.

"Mr. and Mrs. Jeffers haven't checked out. But I don't know if they saw the ghost."

"Let's go ask them!" Dink said. He headed across the lobby.

The man was wearing jeans, hiking boots, and a white sweater.

The woman had black hair and wore a dark blue sweater and faded jeans.

"Hi, Mr. and Mrs. Jeffers," Dink said. "My name is Dink. These are my friends Josh and Ruth Rose. We're investigating the ghost. Did you see it?"

"Why do you want to know?" the man asked.

"Because the hotel owners have hired us to get rid of it!" Ruth Rose said.

"If there really *is* a ghost," Josh muttered.

"There is!" Mrs. Jeffers said. "It scared me half to death!"

"So you saw it?" Dink asked.

"We both did," Mr. Jeffers said, setting down his book. "Last night we played cards down here until about midnight. When we went up to our room, this *thing* appeared out of nowhere!"

Mrs. Jeffers shuddered. "The hallway seemed to grow cold!" she said.

"What did it look like?" Ruth Rose asked.

Mr. Jeffers closed his eyes. "The ghost kind of shimmered as she walked. She had wild-looking white hair and a long glowing robe."

"And black holes instead of eyes!" Mrs. Jeffers added.

"You said 'she,'" Ruth Rose said. "Was it a girl ghost?"

Mr. Jeffers looked at Ruth Rose. "Um, well, I guess so. At least the robe looked like a woman's."

"And you said the ghost 'walked,'" Dink said. "Did it have feet?"

"Feet?" Mr. Jeffers said. "I'm not sure. We hurried right into our room."

Just then Mr. Linkletter came over to the sofa. "Excuse me, Dink," he said. "My uncle is on the phone."

"Mr. Spivets wants to talk to me?" Dink said.

Mr. Linkletter nodded. Dink followed him to the phone.

"Hello?" Dink said. He listened for a few minutes, then hung up and walked back to Josh and Ruth Rose.

"You're not gonna believe this," he said.

"Don't tell me they saw the ghost!" Josh said.

"Nope, but now *we* might," Dink said. "Mr. Spivets wants us to sleep in the hotel tonight!"

CHAPTER 5

Josh and Ruth Rose stared at Dink.

"Honest," Dink said.

"But why?" Ruth Rose asked.

"Since the hotel is almost empty, he said we'd be doing him a favor," Dink said. "If people see us here, they might think the ghost was just a joke."

"Let's do it!" Josh said. "I need a night away from the twins!"

Dink grinned. "Mr. Spivets invited our families, too. And he wants us to investigate the ghost while we're here!"

Josh laughed. "When my little brothers get here, that ghost better watch out!"

By suppertime it was all arranged. The three families would spend the night at the Shangri-la.

Ruth Rose's little brother, Nate, wanted to meet the ghost.

"He'll be my friend!" Nate said. "We can play with my dinosaurs together!"

Dink's family and Ruth Rose's family rode together in one car.

The Pintos' car was already in the parking lot when they arrived. Josh was holding on to his twin brothers, Brian and Bradley. The boys hugged twin teddy bears.

After locking the cars, all twelve of

them trooped into the Shangri-la. Mr. and Mrs. Spivets were waiting in the lobby. They were all dressed up, as if it was a special occasion.

"Good evening, all!" Mr. Spivets said. "Welcome to the Shangri-la!"

The adults shook hands.

"This is very nice of you," Dink's mom told them.

Mrs. Spivets smiled at the kids. "It's the least we can do. These three detectives are going to get to the bottom of this ghost business tonight!"

Dink's father grinned. "As long as they do it before bedtime!"

"Dad," Dink said, rolling his eyes.

Just then Mr. Linkletter joined them. "Where's Casper?" Nate asked him. "I wanna see the ghost!"

Mr. Linkletter blinked at Nate, then handed room keys to Dink, Josh, and Ruth Rose.

"I think you'll find the rooms com-

fortable," he said. "I had rollaway beds brought in for the little ones."

Dink led them all to the elevator.

"What number do you guys have?" Josh asked. "We're in Room 203."

"I'm across the hall," Ruth Rose said, "in 204."

"Me too," Dink said. "202."

Five minutes later, all three families were in their rooms. Dink dumped his backpack on a narrow rollaway bed.

The room was pretty big, with a color TV and a miniature refrigerator. Dink opened the door and found a bunch of soft drinks and snacks.

"Can we eat this stuff?" Dink asked.

His father gave him a look. "You just finished supper, Dinko!"

Dink grinned. "Yeah, I know. How late can I stay up?"

"Nine o'clock," his mother said. "Remember, tomorrow is Monday."

"Mom, tomorrow's Columbus Day!" Dink said, grinning. "No school!"

"Okay, ten o'clock, but not a minute later!"

Dink left the room and knocked on Josh's door. "Come in!" one of the twins yelled.

Dink opened the door. The Pintos' room was even bigger than his. Three small beds were lined up opposite one big one.

Brian and Bradley wore matching Batman jammies and were coloring in their coloring books.

Josh was standing in front of their little fridge, tossing down peanuts.

"Can Josh come out and play?" Dink said, grinning.

Josh's dad said, "Sure, just be back by breakfast time."

Josh laughed. "Let's get Ruth Rose," he said to Dink.

They walked to Room 204 and knocked. Ruth Rose opened the door and stepped out. "My folks are trying to get Nate to go to bed," she whispered.

"Let's go down to the lobby and think of a plan," Dink suggested.

"I already have one!" Ruth Rose announced.

"You do?" Dink said.

Ruth Rose nodded. "Mr. Linkletter told us the ghost showed up at midnight, right? Mr. and Mrs. Jeffers said the same thing."

Josh snorted. "So what's your plan, to hang out and say hi to the ghost when the clock strikes twelve?"

Ruth Rose grinned. "Exactly!"

CHAPTER 6

"It smells awful in here," Josh muttered.

"Josh, this closet is filled with cleaning stuff," Dink told him. "It's *supposed* to smell awful."

"Could you guys whisper?" Ruth Rose said. "You want our parents to wake up and find us gone?"

It was nearly midnight. Ten minutes

before, the kids had snuck out of their rooms and hidden in the closet.

Josh yawned. "I should be asleep, having a great dream," he said. "Instead, I'm squashed in here like a sardine, waiting for a dumb ghost who isn't even real!"

Dink grinned in the dark. "I heard that ghosts hate kids with red hair," he whispered.

"Yeah? Well, I heard that ghosts *eat* blond-haired kids for breakfast!"

Suddenly Ruth Rose put out both hands. "Shh, I think I heard something," she said.

Josh snorted. "Nice try, Ruth Rose, but..."

"Shh!" whispered Dink. "I heard something, too!"

He pushed the closet door open a crack. All three kids peered out into the hallway.

Dink heard a groan, like the wind howling through a cave.

Suddenly a tall white figure appeared at the end of the hall. It gave off a shimmery white light and seemed to float above the floor.

"Oh my gosh!" Josh croaked. "I wanna go back to bed!"

The ghost wore a long white gown. Its hair was white and stuck up in spikes. And there were just black, empty holes where the eyes should have been!

Josh grabbed Dink's arm. It hurt, but Dink was too scared to say anything.

The figure drifted slowly toward the kids' hiding place. It was carrying a long silver sword.

"It knows we're in here!" Josh squeaked.

The ghost paused at each door, then

stopped in front of Room 202.

That's our room! Dink thought.

"Diiiiinnnnk," the ghost moaned. "Goooo hooooome! Thiiiis plaaace is daaaangerous!"

Every hair on Dink's head stood up. He felt cold, as if someone had opened a window.

The ghost floated to the next room.

This time it moaned, *"Josssh, go hooome. Leave before it's toooo laaate!"*

Outside Room 204, the ghost moaned its final message: *"Ruth Rose, take your faaamily and leave nooow!"*

Then the ghost drifted back the way it had come. Seconds later, the hallway was empty.

Ruth Rose jumped up and shoved

the door open. "Come on, let's see where it went!" she said.

"Who cares where it went!" Josh said. "I'm outta here!"

"Come on, Josh," Dink said. "I promised Mr. and Mrs. Spivets we'd get rid of the ghost. And we only have till morning!"

"But what if it gets rid of us instead!"

Dink grabbed Josh's arm and started down the hall. He stopped and listened at Room 202. He heard his father snoring, and grinned.

Suddenly Josh stuck his nose in the air. "What's that smell?" he said.

Dink shrugged and kept walking.

Ruth Rose had reached the end of the hall. "It disappeared," she said when they were standing together.

"I smell it here, too," Josh said.

"Smell what?" Ruth Rose asked.

"I don't know," Josh said. "But it reminds me of something."

Around the corner, the kids found a gray metal door. A red sign on the door read FIRE EXIT.

"Maybe it went through there!" Ruth Rose whispered, pointing at the door.

Dink held his breath, then slowly pushed the door open. The kids peered into the stairwell. They saw dark steps going up and down.

"Should we split up and check it out?" Dink asked.

"No way!" Josh said. "We stick together!"

Dink grinned at his friend. "Still think the ghost is a joke?"

Josh made a face at Dink.

"Guys," Ruth Rose said. "How did the ghost know our names and which rooms we were in?"

"Maybe it has supernatural powers!" Josh said.

"Or maybe the ghost is really someone in the hotel," Dink added. "Someone who knows us!"

Ruth Rose nodded. "I think the ghost came out tonight looking just for us."

"You mean to scare us away, like it did the other people?" Dink asked.

Ruth Rose nodded again.

"Well, it worked!" Josh said. "Let's hit the trail!"

"Hey, what's this?" Ruth Rose asked. She plucked a white hair off the doorframe.

Dink examined the hair. "The ghost had white hair like this," he said.

"Yeah," Ruth Rose said, "but ghosts don't lose hair, *people* do!"

Suddenly the door to Room 204 opened. Ruth Rose's father popped his

head out. "Okay, you guys, time to hit the sack."

"But, Dad, we just..." Ruth Rose said.

Her father shook his head. "Say good night to the boys, Ruth Rose. Now."

CHAPTER 7

By nine the next morning, the three
families were down in the lobby. Ruth
Rose's parents had treated them all to
breakfast at Ellie's Diner, then they'd
walked back to the hotel for their lug-
gage.

While the adults thanked Mr.
Linkletter and the Spivetses, the kids
huddled on the sofa.

"What're we gonna do?" Dink

asked. "Mr. and Mrs. Spivets are selling the hotel today!"

Ruth Rose pulled the white hair from her pocket. "This proves that someone is just pretending to be the ghost," she said. "But we don't know who or why!"

"Maybe one of the guests has white hair," Josh said.

"Josh, all the guests are gone except Mr. and Mrs. Jeffers, and they both have dark hair," Ruth Rose reminded him.

"Could the hair be from a wig?" Dink asked. "The ghost could have been wearing a costume and makeup."

"That's it!" Josh cried. "Last night I smelled makeup in the hall. I remember the yucky smell from last Halloween!"

Just then Mr. Linkletter walked over to the kids. He looked even more unhappy than he had the day before.

"This is a sad day," Mr. Linkletter said. "Eatch, Rail, and Roock will be here at noon with the papers."

"NOON!" Ruth Rose jumped up. "Then we still have three hours!"

Mr. Linkletter gazed down at her. "I'm afraid it's too late." He shook his head and walked away.

"We have to find out who's pretending to be the ghost," Ruth Rose said. "If we don't, Livvy and Mr. Linkletter will lose their jobs!"

"And Mr. and Mrs. Spivets will lose their home!" Dink added.

"Guys, I think I know who the ghost is," Josh said.

Dink and Ruth Rose stared at him.

"Well," Dink said. "Who?"

"The only people left in the hotel are Livvy, Mr. Linkletter, and his aunt and uncle, right?"

"Right," Ruth Rose said.

"And we know that none of them want the hotel to be torn down," Josh continued.

"You forgot about Mr. and Mrs. Jeffers," Dink said. "They're still here."

Josh grinned. "Bingo!"

"The Jefferses?" Ruth Rose said. "But they said they saw the ghost outside their room."

"Sure they saw the ghost," Josh said. "One of them *is* the ghost!"

"I know how we can find out," Dink said. "We have to search their room."

"Mr. Linkletter will never let us do that," Josh said.

"Well, maybe *he* won't let us, but I know someone who might," Ruth Rose said.

"Who?" asked Dink.

"Livvy!"

The kids said good-bye to their families, then hurried to the door that led to the basement.

They found Livvy in a cozy room, drinking a cup of tea. She was wearing her maid's uniform. "'Morning, kids," she said. "What brings you down here?"

"We saw the ghost last night!" Ruth Rose said.

Livvy's eyes widened. "Really? Where? Tell me!"

The kids explained about spending the night in the hotel and hiding in the cleaning closet.

"It was so creepy!" Josh said. "First we heard all these weird noises, then this thing came out of nowhere!"

"It glowed!" Ruth Rose said. She showed Livvy the white hair. "And we found this!"

"We think the ghost is one of the guests wearing a costume and wig," Dink explained.

Suddenly Livvy let out a gasp. "It was a *wig!*" she cried.

"What was?" Ruth Rose asked.

"I just remembered," Livvy said. "Yesterday I was in 301 getting ready to vacuum. When I looked under the bed for shoes and stuff, I saw this hairy white thing. I thought it was a rat. But it could have been a white wig!"

"Who's in Room 301?" Dink asked.

Livvy shrugged. "I don't know their name, but they're a nice couple from New York."

"Could you let us in so we could check the room for clues?" Ruth Rose asked.

Livvy shook her head. "Sorry, but you know how Mr. Linkletter is about the guests' privacy."

"But Mr. and Mrs. Spivets hired us to get rid of the ghost!" Dink said. "Besides, if they have to sell the hotel, you and Mr. Linkletter will lose your jobs!"

"And Mr. and Mrs. Spivets will have to move," Ruth Rose added. "Please, Livvy? It won't take us long."

Livvy took a moment to think. "Okay," she finally said. "But just for two minutes!"

"Hey, what's this?" Josh had stuck his head into a small opening in one wall.

"That's an old dumbwaiter," Livvy explained. "In the old days, the hotel sent food up to the guests. Each room had one of these little elevator things. When the food got up there, the guests just opened a door and pulled out their food tray."

"Our room didn't have one," Dink said.

"None of them do anymore," Livvy said. "When the hotel closed its kitchen, the dumbwaiters were all sealed up."

She pointed to the one in her wall. "That's the only hole left."

Josh stuck his head back into the opening. "Cool! This thing goes way up!"

"Right," Livvy explained. "The shaft is still there, but the openings into the rooms were covered over."

Josh yelled "Hello!" into the empty shaft. His voice came echoing back.

Livvy finished her tea. "Okay, let's go," she said. "I'll be glad when Mr. Linkletter is back to normal again. He's even grouchier than usual!"

Livvy took the kids up to the third floor, then knocked at Room 301. When no one answered, she unlocked the door and pushed it open.

"Please don't touch anything," she said. She knelt down and peeked under both beds. "The wig's gone!"

The kids looked around the room. "Maybe it's in the closet!" Ruth Rose whispered.

Livvy pulled open the closet door. On the top shelf sat a plastic head wearing a spiky white wig.

"That's it!" Josh said.

"Can you take it down?" Dink asked.

Livvy carefully took the head down and set it on a table.

Ruth Rose removed the white hair from her pocket and held it next to the wig.

"The hairs are the same!" she said.

CHAPTER 8

"Look." Dink pointed to a small framed picture on the bedside table. "Mr. and Mrs. Jeffers!"

"You know these people?" Livvy asked.

"We met them yesterday," Ruth Rose said. "We think one of them might be the ghost."

Livvy's eyes grew wide. "Why

would they want to scare the guests away? They seem so nice!"

"That's what we plan to find out," Dink said.

Livvy carefully placed the wig back on the closet shelf.

As she stepped back, her arm caught on something. A long silver object clunked to the floor.

"It's the ghost's sword!" Ruth Rose said. She picked it up and laughed. "It's just painted wood!"

"Guys, look at this stuff!" Josh had been examining some tubes and bottles on a vanity table. "Look, white clown makeup. And black! This is what I smelled in the hallway last night!"

"Hey, guys, a tape recorder," Ruth Rose said.

"Kids, please don't touch..."

Before Livvy could finish, Ruth Rose had pushed the PLAY button.

Suddenly the room was filled with spooky noises. Livvy and the kids listened as a voice moaned and groaned.

"Those are the same noises we heard last night!" Dink said.

"Have you seen Mr. and Mrs. Jeffers this morning?" Ruth Rose asked Livvy.

Livvy shook her head. "Maybe they went out for breakfast." She looked at her watch. "And I have to get busy."

Livvy locked the door behind them,

and they all got in the elevator.

"Thanks for letting us in," Ruth Rose said to Livvy.

Livvy put one finger to her lips. "Let's keep this a secret, okay?" she whispered. "From you-know-who!"

"It's a deal," Ruth Rose whispered back.

The elevator door opened and Livvy left the kids in the lobby.

"There's Mr. Linkletter," Josh said.

"Maybe he knows where Mr. and Mrs. Jeffers went."

The kids walked over to the front desk.

Mr. Linkletter looked as if he hadn't been to bed. His suit was rumpled, and his hair stuck up in the back.

"Maybe we shouldn't disturb him," Ruth Rose whispered.

"But we have to find Mr. and Mrs. Jeffers," Dink said. "We don't have much more time!"

Dink walked up to the desk and put on his best smile. "Hi, Mr. Linkletter!"

Mr. Linkletter gazed down at Dink. "Oh, hello," he said.

"Do you happen to know where Mr. and Mrs. Jeffers are this morning?" he asked.

Mr. Linkletter waved his hand toward the door. "They told me they were going to Ellie's for breakfast."

"Thanks, Mr. Linkletter!" Dink said.

The kids left the hotel and hurried up Main Street toward Ellie's Diner.

"What're we gonna say to them?" Josh asked. "We can't just walk up and accuse them of being the ghost, can we?"

Ruth Rose pushed open the door to the diner. "Don't worry," she said. "I have a plan."

Ellie was behind the counter, mixing tuna salad in a big bowl. She waved as the kids sat in one of the booths.

"There they are," Josh whispered. He nodded his head toward another booth, where Mr. and Mrs. Jeffers were eating breakfast.

"They look so nice," Dink said. "Not like people who would try to ruin a hotel."

Ellie came to their booth. "Back so soon?" she asked, opening her pad.

"Don't tell me you're having another breakfast!"

"Can I borrow your pad and pencil?" Ruth Rose asked.

Ellie gave Ruth Rose a sly smile and handed them over. "What are you kids up to?" she asked.

"I'll give them back in a minute," Ruth Rose said.

"Okey-dokey, I'll see you in a minute then," Ellie said, heading back to her tuna salad.

Ruth Rose began writing.

"What're you doing?" Josh asked.

"Wait a sec!" Ruth Rose said. She finished and pushed the pad in front of Dink and Josh. "What do you think?"

DEAR MR. AND MRS. JEFFERS,
WE KNOW ALL ABOUT THE
WHITE WIG AND THE
TAPE RECORDER.
GUESS WHO!

"Ruth Rose! What if we're wrong about the Jefferses?" Dink asked.

"We're not wrong," Ruth Rose said, getting up.

She walked over to Ellie, said something to her, and handed her the pad. Ellie smiled at Ruth Rose, then headed for the Jefferses' booth.

Ruth Rose hurried back and sat down. "Now watch," she told Dink and Josh.

They watched as Ellie handed the note to Mrs. Jeffers.

Mrs. Jeffers read the note, then said something to Ellie. Ellie pointed toward the kids.

Mrs. Jeffers waved, and Ruth Rose waved back.

"Come on," Ruth Rose said. She walked over to the Jefferses' booth. Dink and Josh were right behind her.

"Hi!" Ruth Rose said, pulling the

white hair from her pocket. "I think your wig got caught on the fire door last night. You left this."

She placed the white hair on the green place mat.

Mrs. Jeffers stared at the hair, then at the kids. Finally she looked at her husband.

Mr. Jeffers sighed, then grinned at the kids. "Looks like you got us!" he said.

CHAPTER 9

"So you really *are* the ghost?" Ruth Rose asked.

Mr. Jeffers nodded. "That was me last night," he said. "Cindy here was the ghost the first two nights."

He looked at the kids. "Weren't you asleep in your rooms when I came by?"

"We hid in a smelly closet and saw you!" Josh said.

Mr. Jeffers smiled. "Do I make a good ghost?"

"You sure scared me!" Josh said.

"But why did you do it?" Ruth Rose asked.

"We're both actors, and we're broke," Mrs. Jeffers said. "A few weeks ago, three men came up to us after a rehearsal and asked if we wanted a job."

"So we told them sure!" her husband said. "The men told us to check into the Shangri-la and scare the guests away. We came up with the ghost costume ourselves."

"How do you make it glow?" Josh asked.

"I glued a string of tiny lights inside the gown," Mrs. Jeffers said. "The battery was under the wig."

Her husband smiled. "And I thought of hiding the tape recorder in the basement dumbwaiter. The noise went all through the hotel walls!"

"But that's so mean!" Ruth Rose said. "If the hotel closes, what will happen to Mr. Linkletter and Livvy and Mr. and Mrs. Spivets?"

Mr. Jeffers put up his hands. "Who said anything about the hotel closing?"

"Mr. and Mrs. Spivets did," Dink said. "They're selling the hotel because of you!"

"What?" Mrs. Jeffers said. "But Mr. and Mrs. Spivets are supposed to know all about the ghost act. So is Mr. Linkletter."

"Look," said Mr. Jeffers. "The three guys who hired us told us that the hotel is going to be used in a horror movie. Scaring guests away is supposed to be great publicity. All the guests are going to get their money back, plus free passes to the movie."

"And we're supposed to get starring parts in the movie!" his wife said. "It's a big break for us!"

The kids looked at each other.

"But Mr. and Mrs. Spivets don't know anything about any movie," Ruth Rose said. "Neither does Mr. Linkletter. They're really upset because they're going to have to sell the hotel. Today!"

"Yeah," Josh said. "Mrs. Spivets was crying and everything!"

"We even saw the letter from the real estate company," Dink said. "Their names were something like Peach or Roach."

"Eatch, Rail, and Roock?" Mr. Jeffers suddenly asked.

"That's them!" Dink said. "They've been trying to buy the hotel for a long time, but Mr. Spivets refused to sell. Until now."

Mr. Jeffers looked at his wife. "Oh,

no," he said. "Eatch, Rail, and Roock are the men who hired us!"

His wife had gone from happy to sad. "No wonder they told us not to talk to Mr. Linkletter about the movie. There never *was* one!"

Her husband shook his head. "All they wanted was the hotel—and we helped them get it!"

"I feel terrible," Mrs. Jeffers said. She turned to her husband. "Todd, isn't there anything we can do?"

Mr. Jeffers looked at the kids. "Do you think it's too late?" he asked. "Have they actually sold the hotel yet?"

Dink glanced at the clock over the counter. "They're signing the papers at noon," he said. "But I think I know how you can get rid of Eatch, Rail, and Roock and save the hotel at the same time!"

CHAPTER 10

"This wig itches!" Josh complained. He, Dink, and Ruth Rose were hiding behind the desk in the hotel lobby.

Josh was dressed as the ghost, complete with wig, robe, and makeup.

"It won't be long now," Dink said, glancing at the clock. It was almost noon!

"Eatch, Rail, and Roock had better

hurry up," Josh said. "I'm gonna suffocate in this dumb dress!"

From where he was hiding, Dink could see the rest of the lobby. Mr. Linkletter was sitting on the sofa with his aunt and uncle.

On the other side of the lobby, Mr. and Mrs. Jeffers were playing cards with Linda Gomez, the reporter from the *Green Lawn Gazette*. Next to her sat a man with a camera.

"What if they don't come?" Ruth Rose whispered.

Dink smiled and pointed at the front door. "I think they just did!"

Three men walked into the lobby. One was tall, one was medium, and one was short and round. Each was dressed in a dark suit, white shirt, and blue tie.

"They look like three penguins!" Josh said.

Mr. Linkletter hurried over to the

men, then led them back to his aunt and uncle.

The tall man shook hands with Mr. Spivets. "I am Fletcher Eatch," he said.

"I am Randolph Rail," the medium-sized man said, sticking out his hand.

"And I am Miles Roock," the short man said, shaking hands in turn.

Mr. Spivets nodded at the men. "Have you brought the papers?" he asked.

Fletcher Eatch beamed. "We certainly have!" he said. He handed Mr. Spivets an important-looking document.

Randolph Rail removed an envelope from his briefcase. "And here's the check."

Miles Roock whipped a gold pen out

of his pocket. "All we need is your signature, Mr. Spivets," he said.

Mr. Spivets looked sadly at his wife. Then he took the pen and started to sign the document.

Just then Mr. and Mrs. Jeffers walked up.

"Look, Todd!" Mrs. Jeffers said. "It's the movie producers!"

"What a surprise," her husband said. "We were just talking about the movie you're going to film here in the hotel!"

Mr. Spivets paused. "What's this about a movie?" he asked suspiciously.

"Um..." began Fletcher Eatch.

"Well..." started Randolph Rail.

"W-we can explain!" said Miles Roock.

"There's no need to explain," said Linda Gomez. She stood up and walked toward the men. "I'm a reporter from the *Green Lawn Gazette.* Tomorrow my column will tell the whole town how you tried to trick these people into selling their hotel!"

The three men stared at Linda, then at the Jefferses. Finally their eyes landed on Mr. and Mrs. Spivets.

Fletcher Eatch turned pink.

Randolph Rail went white.

Miles Roock turned purple. There was dead silence in the Shangri-la lobby.

And then a ghost in a spiky white wig floated up from behind the desk. *"Go hooome,"* it moaned in a creepy voice. *"Go home before it's toooo laaate!"*

Everyone in the lobby—except Eatch, Rail, and Roock—started to laugh.

"I guess I won't be needing this," Mr. Spivets said. He ripped the document he was holding into pieces.

"W-what are you doing!" Fletcher Eatch spluttered.

"You agreed to sell this hotel!" Randolph Rail said.

"You can't back out of a deal with Eatch, Rail, and Roock!" said Miles Roock.

Mrs. Spivets stood up next to her husband.

"Eatch, Rail, and Roock?" she said. "You should rearrange the letters in

your names to Cheat, Liar, and Crook!"

"And now," Mr. Spivets said, "I think it's time for you gentlemen to leave."

Without another word, Mr. Linkletter escorted the three men to the front door.

The man with the camera followed,

snapping one picture after another.

Everyone cheered. Flo Spivets cheered the loudest.

Mrs. Jeffers turned back to Mr. and Mrs. Spivets. "My husband and I are so sorry for what we did," she said. "Can you ever forgive us?"

"Of course we can, dear," Mrs. Spivets said.

"In fact," said Mr. Spivets, "you were such good ghosts, we'd like to invite you to do it again! One weekend a month, we'd like you to put on a 'Shangri-la Mystery' for our guests. What do you think?"

"That's a great idea," Mr. Jeffers said. "We can get some of our actor friends to help!"

The photographer snapped pictures of the Jefferses and the Spivetses.

"Wait till my readers hear about this!" Linda Gomez said, writing it all down on her pad.

Then Mr. Spivets turned to Dink, Josh, and Ruth Rose. "And speaking of mysteries, I want to thank our three super sleuths!"

He pulled three envelopes out of his pocket. "From the bottom of our hearts, Mrs. Spivets and I thank you," he said. He handed the envelopes to the kids. "Please open these before you go to bed."

The photographer snapped a picture as the kids blushed.

"Be sure to mention their names in the column," Mrs. Spivets said to Linda Gomez.

"My pleasure," Linda said. "Now, how about a few more pictures of the three kids?"

Dink and Ruth Rose looked into the camera and smiled.

"Wait!" Josh said, struggling out of the ghost costume. "I don't want picture in the paper with thi dress on!"

*　　*　　*

Later that night, the kids met in Dink's living room.

Dink was holding Loretta in his lap. She was nibbling on one of his shirt buttons.

Josh pulled out the envelope Mr. Spivets had given him. "Can we open these now?" he asked.

"He said before we go to bed, Josh," Dink said.

"This *is* before we go to bed!"

"Josh is right!" Ruth Rose said. "I'm dying to know what's in mine. Let's open them on the count of three, okay? One, two, three!"

my great-aunt Molly!"

ree plane tickets to

d up the contents of

d three passes to

Dink gulped when he saw what was in his envelope. He pulled out three fifty-dollar bills and a note:

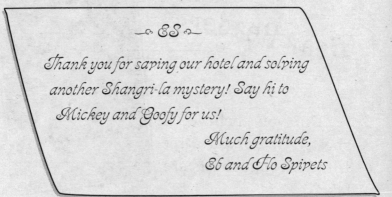

— ⚬ ℰ𝒮 ⚬ —

Thank you for saving our hotel and solving another Shangri-la mystery! Say hi to Mickey and Goofy for us!

Much gratitude,
Eb and Flo Spivets

Dink, Josh, and Ruth Rose jumped up and did a triple high-five.

Loretta crawled off the sofa. No one was looking, so she started chewing one of the fifty-dollar bills.

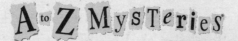

A to Z Mysteries

Dear Readers,

Do you believe in ghosts? Or do you agree with Josh that ghosts are fake?

While researching this book, I talked with lots of people who said they had seen ghosts. One woman told me that her husband's ghost visits her every day at four o'clock. That was when they had tea when he was still alive.

One boy told me about how his grandfather always used to take him fishing. Now, whenever he goes fishing, the boy sees his grandfather's ghost.

If there are ghosts, I think they are friendly. Maybe they get lonely, and that's why they visit the people they love. Do *you* know any ghost stories? I'd love to hear them!

Please visit my Web site at www.ronroy.com or send your letters to:

Ron Roy
c/o Random House Children's Books
1745 Broadway, Mail Drop 11-2
New York, NY 10019

Happy reading!

Spookily yours,

Ron Roy

Collect clues with Dink, Josh, and Ruth Rose in their next exciting adventure,

THE INVISIBLE ISLAND

Dink took a step forward, then stopped. His jaw dropped.

"What's in there?" Josh asked.

Dink didn't answer.

"Dink?" Ruth Rose said. "What's going on?"

Dink gulped and tried to speak. "Muh—muh—muh—"

"What the heck is 'muh'?" Josh said. "Mud? Mummies? Muffins?"

Dink could barely breathe, let alone talk. He swallowed again.

"Money!" he finally said.